The Christmas Fairy

To the lovely Haynes family – Emma, Stuart,
Amy, Charlie, Saffron and Theo, and
in loving memory of Hattie – A.B.

To Elsa, Ella and Maria. Love from Rosi B x

First published in 2016 by Nosy Crow Ltd

The Crow's Nest, 10a Lant Street

London SE1 1QR

www.nosycrow.com

ISBN 978 0 85763 411 5 (HB)

ISBN 978 0 85763 705 5 (PB)

A CIP catalogue record for this book is available
from the British Library.

Printed in China by Imago
Papers used by Nosy Crow are made from wood grown in sustainable forests.

1 3 5 7 9 8 6 4 2 (HB)

1 3 5 7 9 8 6 4 2 (PB)

The Christmas Fairy

Anne Booth

Illustrated by

Rosalind Beardshaw

nosy crow

Clara was a chatterbox,
a fairy full of fun.
She loved to sing and dance
and bring a smile to everyone.

And every day at fairy school
she wished that she could be
a proper Christmas fairy
on a sparkly Christmas tree.

So Clara was excited
when she heard Miss Petal call,
"It's **Christmas fairy** lesson time –
I'm going to teach you all!

You'll learn to stand like statues while you hold a **fairy** pose,
and stay as **quiet** as a mouse whilst standing on your toes.

And then you must be **sensible** – don't wave your wands around.
Now Clara, listen **carefully**,
and **please** don't make a sound."

"We'll practise hard all term
and then you'll show me what you know.
And afterwards I'll take you to
a **special** Christmas Show.

You'll see a bluebird singer with a **lovely** cheerful song,
and some **very** funny penguin clowns are going to come along.

Next a **graceful** ballerina swan will dance and pirouette.

I'm sure the Christmas Show this year is one we **won't** forget!"

"But first," Miss Petal said,
"you'll practise standing in your pose.
Remember to stay very still
and not to scratch your nose."

So Clara balanced on one leg,
but gave a little giggle . . .

. . . which turned into a **wobble** and
became a **great big wriggle!**

"Now fairies," said Miss Petal,
"stay as quiet as can be.
And think how **happy** you will feel
when you are on a tree."

So Clara tried her **very** best, but somehow it went wrong . . .
Her quiet happy thoughts became a **hum** and then a **song!**

"Be sensible," Miss Petal said, "and form a crocodile."

"A real one?" giggled Clara,

which made all the others smile.

"Or maybe," Clara said, "we could all form a tall giraffe!"

"Oh, come on girls!" Miss Petal sighed.

"This is no time to laugh."

Then just before the Christmas Show,
Miss Petal set a test.
"Let's all be **Christmas** fairies now.
Please try your **very** best.

I'd like to see you hold your poses, silent, still and calm."
And Clara tried ... but got the giggles **and** an itchy arm!

Miss Petal sighed, "That's not at all
what Christmas fairies do.
You always sing, or dance, or laugh.
What **shall** I do with you?"

And when the fairies formed a line
and set off for the show,
poor Clara dawdled at the back,
her footsteps **very** slow.

"I'll **never** be a proper fairy on a Christmas tree.
I'm a noisy, wriggly, giggler and I **wish** I wasn't me."

But then she heard a jingling sound,
looked up and saw a sleigh.
"Ho ho there, Clara," Santa cried.
"I'm landing now, make way!"

"We **need** you Clara," Santa said,
"that's why I've come along.
The Christmas Show's in trouble –
almost **everything's**
gone wrong."

"The little bluebird's lost his voice
and **cannot** make a sound.

The ballerina **bumped**
her head whilst whirling
round and round.

The penguin clowns were on the ice and had a **nasty** fall.
If no one takes their places there will be no show **at all!**"

"We need a special fairy who is full of life and fun,
who dances, sings, and laughs and jokes
and cheers up everyone.

You're such a happy fairy,
and you always let it show.
You make us smile, no matter what,
so would you have a go?"

"Who **me?**" said little Clara.

"Can I **really** play each part?"

"Of course you can," said Santa,

"and the show's about to start!"

So Clara stepped on to the stage
and sang a Christmas song.
And **everybody** watching clapped
their hands and sang along.

Next Clara stretched her arms out wide
and **twirled** across the floor
so fast the audience all gasped and
loudly cheered for more!

Then Clara made the fairies laugh
(and all the others, too)
by **trumpeting** and **roaring**
like the creatures in a zoo.

When Clara finished, everyone stood up and gave three cheers,
and Santa boomed, "Your Christmas show's
the **best** I've seen for years!

Some Christmas fairies make us sing
and laugh, and so you see,
not **every** Christmas fairy
has to stand still on a tree.

Oh, well done, Clara," Santa said.
"You **really** saved the show.
And I've a gift for everyone –
it's out here in the snow."

He led them to a Christmas tree,
so beautiful and green.
"Oh, thank you," whispered Clara.
"It's the **best** I've ever seen."

And all the fairies climbed
into the branches of the tree,
with Clara on the very top,
as **happy** as could be.